Home Sweet Home

A Story About Safety At Home

Written by
Cindy Leaney

Illustrated by
Peter Wilks

Rourke
Publishing LLC
Vero Beach, Florida 32964

Before you read this story, take a look at the front cover of the book. Emily and Makayla are at the computer.

1. What do you think they are doing?

2. And how do you think this might have something to do with safety at home?

Produced by SGA Illustration and Design
Designed by Phil Kay
Series Editor: Frank Sloan

www.rourkepublishing.com

Library of Congress Cataloging-in-Publication Data

Leaney, Cindy.
   Home sweet home : safety at home / by Cindy Leaney ; illustrated by Peter Wilks.
     p. cm. -- (Hero club safety)
   Summary: When Emily goes to Makayla's house after school, she learns
about being safe on the way there and protecting herself from strangers.

   ISBN 1-58952-740-2
   1. Safety education--Juvenile literature. [1. Safety. 2. Strangers.]
   I. Wilks, Peter, ill. II. Title. III. Series.

HQ770.7.L42 2003
613.6'071--dc21

                                        2003000438

Printed in the USA
MP/W

Welcome to The Hero Club!
Read about all the things that happen to them.
Try and guess what they'll do next.

www.theheroclub.com

"I'm glad your mom said you could come home with me after school."

"Me too."

"What time does your mom get home?"

"Not until 5:30. But I've got a key.
We can watch TV or play on
the computer."

"Cool."

"Why don't we go this way? It's shorter, isn't it?"

"A little, but Mom and Dad and I have a special route. If I'm late, they know where to look for me."

"Hey. Look at the girl by the car. She's the new girl in first grade. She lives near us. That's not her dad!"

"You're lucky Makayla and Emily saw you. You should never talk to anyone you don't know."

"He asked me for directions."

"A stranger is a stranger."

"Why are you looking around?"

"I do it to make sure everything's normal."

"I just have to call Mrs. Ames and then I'll get us some milk and cookies."

"Let's play on the computer.
I know a cool website."

21

"This is neat. Look at all
these activities."

"Let's check out the chat room.
What's your screen name?"

"K-Lo."

"This is a great contest. You just send a picture of yourself with your name and address."

"Huh? What do you mean?"

"You should never give out private stuff on the Net. Strangers are strangers. We'd better tell a grown-up."

WHAT DO YOU THINK?

Why do you think Makayla's family has an "after school system?" What are some of the things Makayla does as part of the system?

IMPORTANT IDEAS

On page 12 the playground monitor says, "A stranger is a stranger." Then, on page 26, Makayla says the same thing to Emily about giving out private stuff on the Internet.

What do you do to stay safe on the Internet?

Now that you have read this book, see if you can answer these questions:

1. What are Emily and Makayla planning to do after school and where are they going?

2. Why do Emily and Makayla decide not to take a shorter route to Makayla's house?

3. Why are the girls upset when they see a first grader talking to someone in a car?

4. Why does Makayla call Mrs. Ames?

About the author

Cindy Leaney teaches English and writes books for both young readers and adults. She has lived and worked in England, Kenya, Mexico, Saudi Arabia, and the United States.

About the illustrator

Peter Wilks began work in advertising, where he developed a love for illustration. He has drawn pictures for many children's books in Great Britain and in the United States.

HERO CLUB SAFETY SERIES

Do You Smell Smoke? (A Book About Safety with Fire)

Help! I Can't Swim! (A Book About Safety in Water)

Home Sweet Home (A Book About Safety at Home)

Long Walk to School (A Book About Bullying)

Look Out! (A Book About Safety on Bicycles)

Wrong Stop (A Book About Safety from Crime)